Yun
of the
Ice Spirit

Written by Charlotte Raby

Illustrated by Simona Sanfilippo

One dark day, Yun was on his way home. "Nothing ever happens in my village," he sighed. He didn't know that *everything* was about to change!

As Yun plodded up the hill, he heard a strange noise. "That's odd," he said to himself. "I wonder if a goat is stuck."

Then he heard a soft cry.

"Help! Over here!"

Yun saw a girl tied to a tree.

"Don't touch the ropes!" said the girl. "They are magic! If you touch them, the Ice Spirit will know. He's asleep in the cave."

"Why are you tied up?" he whispered to the girl.

"The Ice Spirit is my father's enemy," she said. "I am the Dragon Princess, daughter of the Dragon King. The Ice Spirit wants to kill me! Please go and tell my father. Swim down to his palace under the lake."

"Of course!" said Yun. "But I can't breathe under the water, so how will I get to the palace?"

"Take my necklace," the princess whispered. "It will help you!"

Yun stood by the clear water of the lake and put on the necklace. He was afraid, but he dived in.

Yun could breathe under the water!
He swam deeper and deeper ...
until he saw the Crystal Palace of the
Dragon King.

In front of the palace were three giant crabs.

"I want to see the Dragon King," said Yun. "I have some news about his daughter."

The crabs led Yun into the palace and up to a golden door. The door opened ... and there stood an old man.

Yun stared. "Are you the Dragon King?" he asked.

The old man nodded.

"The Ice Spirit has your daughter," said Yun.

The old man began to shake.
Then he let out a great roar and
changed into a huge, red dragon!

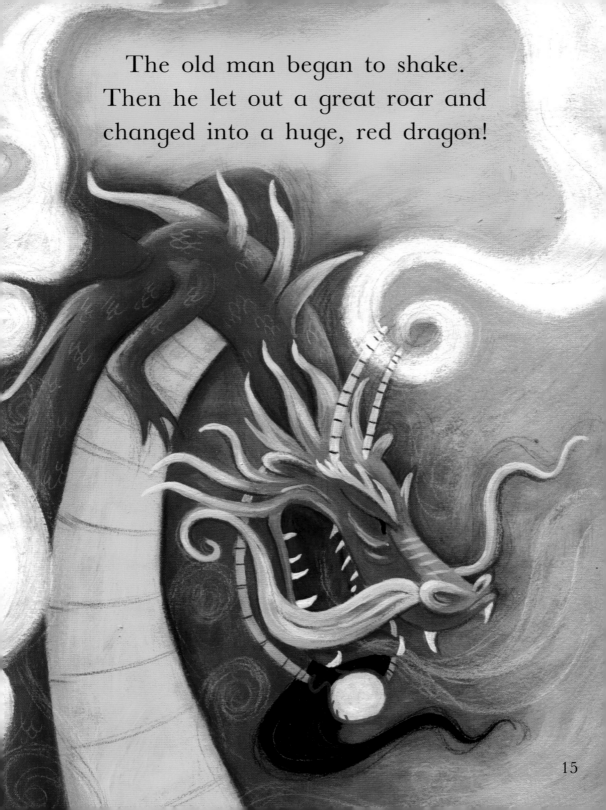

"I can show you the way," said Yun. The Dragon King lowered his head and Yun climbed onto his back.

They flew through the lake and burst
out of the water, up into the air.

When they reached the cave, the
Dragon King rushed inside with a roar.

The Dragon King and the Ice Spirit were fighting hard. Yun cut the magic ropes. The Dragon Princess was free!

At once, the Dragon Princess turned into
a white dragon and joined her father in
the fight. But they needed Yun's help.

Yun grabbed two sticks and rubbed them together. He made fire! He threw the burning sticks at the Ice Spirit. The Ice Spirit roared in anger, hissed ... and melted!

At the palace, the Dragon King changed back into an old man. "You have done well, Yun," he said. He gave Yun a blue dragon charm with ruby eyes.

The Dragon King smiled. "Yun," he said, "this charm will give you dragon powers. With it, you have the power to breathe underwater. You can use the charm to call me at any time."

"If you are brave and kind," said the Dragon King, "you will unlock more powers. When you have unlocked them all, you will be able to change into a dragon whenever you wish!"